Copyright © 2004 by Michael Neugebauer Verlag AG,
Gossau Zürich, Switzerland
First published in Switzerland under the title *Grosser Pauli, kleiner Pauli*.
English translation copyright © 2004 by North-South Books Inc., New York

First published in the United States, Great Britain, Canada, Australia,
and New Zealand in 2004 by North-South Books, an imprint
of Nord-Süd Verlag AG, Gossau Zürich, Switzerland.
Distributed in the United States by North-South Books Inc., New York.

Library of Congress Cataloging-in-Publication Data is available.
A CIP catalogue record for this book is available from The British Library.
ISBN 0-7358-1933-5 (trade edition) 10 9 8 7 6 5 4 3 2 1
ISBN 0-7358-1934-3 (library edition) 10 9 8 7 6 5 4 3 2 1
Printed in Italy

For more information about our books, and the authors and artists
who create them, visit our web site: www.northsouth.com

Davy
in the Middle

Brigitte Weninger
Illustrated by Eve Tharlet

A MICHAEL NEUGEBAUER BOOK
NORTH-SOUTH BOOKS / NEW YORK / LONDON

Tap, tap, tap . . .

Davy woke up and rubbed his eyes. "Dan, where are you going?" he whispered sleepily to his brother.

"I'm going hiking on the mountain," Dan whispered back.

"Great! I'll come with you," said Davy.

But Dan shook his head. "You're still too small for that, Davy."

"Oh, all right," mumbled Davy, slipping back under the covers.

When Davy came into the kitchen, Father Rabbit was playing hop-on-pop with Daisy, Donny, and Dinah who were shrieking and giggling.

"I want to play too!" shouted Davy.

But Father shook his head. "You're too big for this game, Davy."

"Oh, all right," said Davy with a sigh.

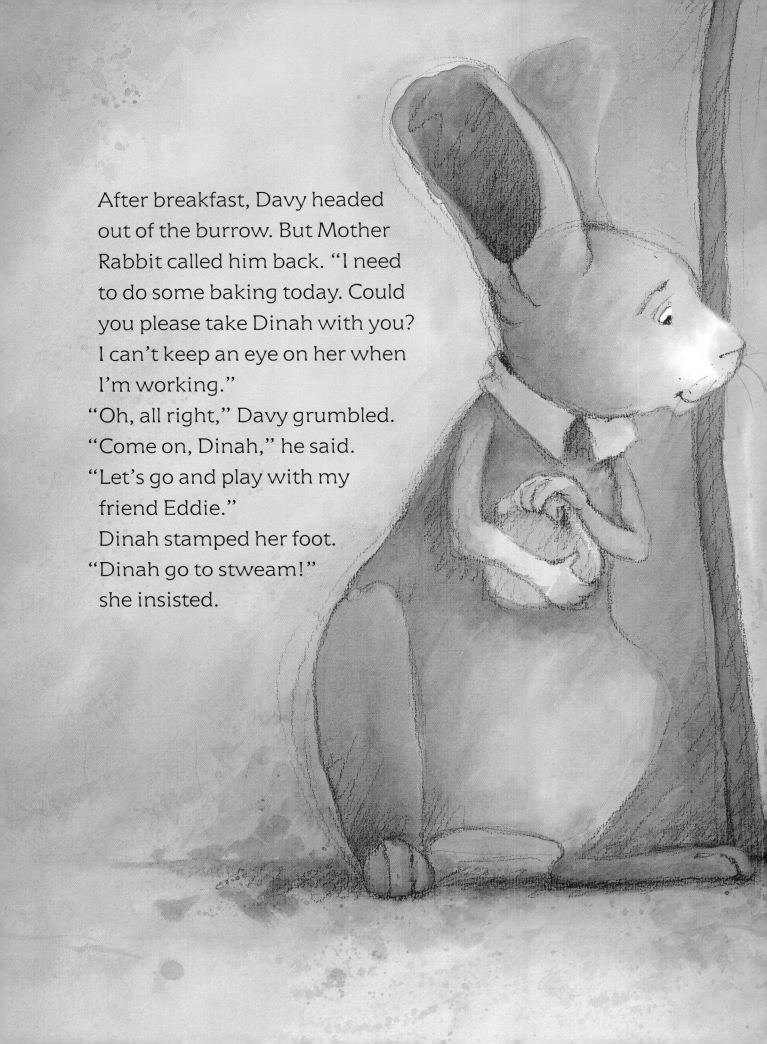

After breakfast, Davy headed
out of the burrow. But Mother
Rabbit called him back. "I need
to do some baking today. Could
you please take Dinah with you?
I can't keep an eye on her when
I'm working."
"Oh, all right," Davy grumbled.
"Come on, Dinah," he said.
"Let's go and play with my
friend Eddie."
Dinah stamped her foot.
"Dinah go to stweam!"
she insisted.

Davy had had enough.

"That's it! Why can't I ever do what *I* want?" he wailed.

Dinah was startled and started to cry.

Davy felt ashamed. "I'm sorry," he said, giving her a big hug. "It's not your fault. Come on, we'll go to the stream. And we'll build a big mud castle, okay?"

Dinah sniffed and nodded.

When Davy and Dinah came back home, Mother was still baking. "Gracious!" she exclaimed. "You're filthy! Davy, could you help Dinah wash up?"

"No!" snapped Davy. "Let someone else do it!" He ran out and slammed the door behind him.

"What on earth is wrong with him?" asked Mother, shocked. Dinah shrugged, then hurried after her big brother.

Davy ran to his secret hideout.

"Oh rotten carrots!" he grumbled. "I'm NEVER allowed to do what I want. I'm too small or too big to do anything fun, but whenever anyone needs me to do something for them, I'm just right."

Davy started to cry. "Nobody loves me!" he wailed.

Nicky, his toy rabbit, listened sympathetically. Davy wiped his tears with Nicky's soft paws.

Excitedly, Dinah ran back to
the burrow.
"Mother! Father!" she called.
"Davy's cwying! He says no
one wuvs him!"
"What's wrong with him today?"
asked Mother, worried.

"Hmmm, I think I might know," said Father.
"It's not easy being Davy. He's stuck in the middle—
too big for some things, too little for others."

Mother Rabbit nodded. "That's true. And whenever we need something, he's the one we go to first, because he's always so helpful."

"Maybe we should just tell Davy that we *do* love him," said Dan.

"Great idea," shouted Daisy. "And I'll decorate his place at the table. Maybe that will cheer him up."

"Dinah make Davy pwesent," declared Dinah.

"I'll give him a present too," said Donny. "And afterward, we can eat Mother's delicious cake!"

"Oh boy, this is going to be some party!" laughed Father. "Come on, let's get started!"

A little later, Dinah crawled into Davy's hideout.

"Come, Davy," she called, taking his paw.

"*Now* what," grumbled Davy, following along reluctantly.

The whole Rabbit family greeted him at the door, calling out,
"Hooray! Davy's back. Now the party can begin!"

"Bu—bu—it's not my birthday!" stammered Davy.

"No, it's a special party." Mother smiled. "A thank-you party!"

Mother hugged Davy. "Thank you, Davy, for all your help."
Then Father Rabbit said, "Thank you, Davy. You may be too big for some things and too little for others, but to me you're just right."
Dan gave him a special bird feather. "Thank you, Davy, for being a big brother with me."

"Thanks for all the funny ideas you always have," said Daisy.
"With you around, we're never bored."
"That's what I wanted to say," said Donny. He gave Davy a
  beautiful snail shell.
Dinah gave him a big kiss and said, "Davy is da gweatest!"

Davy glowed as brightly as Daisy's sunflower. "Thank you!" he said, smiling. Then Davy jumped up and plopped Dinah down on his beautifully decorated chair. "Now we're all going to say thank you to Dinah and tell *her* why she's special! And then everyone gets a turn on the chair!"

Father laughed. "Another great Davy-idea! But we'd better eat Mother's cake first—this may be a pretty long party!"

"Yes!" said Davy happily. "It's going to be long and fun and wonderful."
And it was.